W9-COZ-578

AUTOMOBILE

204 N Cascade, PO Box 717
Fergus Falls, MN 56538-0717

26 letters and 99 cents

BY TANA HOBAN

A MULBERRY PAPERBACK BOOK, NEW YORK

This one is for Candace

Soft Touch letters and numbers used in this book are available
at most toy stores.

The photographs were reproduced from 35-mm slides and
printed in full color.

The Library of Congress has cataloged the Greenwillow Books
edition of 26 Letters and 99 Cents as follows: Hoban, Tana.
26 letters and 99 cents. Summary: Color photographs of
letters, numbers, coins, and common objects introduce
the alphabet, coinage, and the counting system.
ISBN 0-688-06361-6 ISBN 0-688-06362-4 (lib. bdg.)
1. English language—Alphabet—Juvenile literature.
2. Counting—Juvenile literature. [1. Alphabet.
2. Counting. 3. Coins] I. Title. II. Title: Twenty-six
letters and ninety-nine cents.
PE1155.H57 1987 [E] 86-11993

10 9 8 7 6 5 4
First Mulberry Edition, 1995
ISBN 0-688-14389-X

Aa

Bb

Cc

Dd

E e

F f

Gg

Hh

I i

J j

Kk

Ll

Mm

Nn

O o

P p

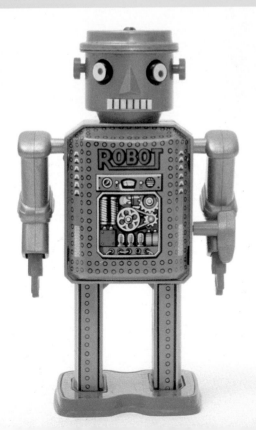

Ss

Tt

U u

V v

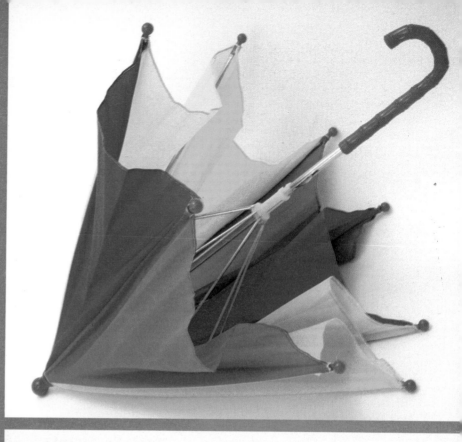

BE MY VALENTINE

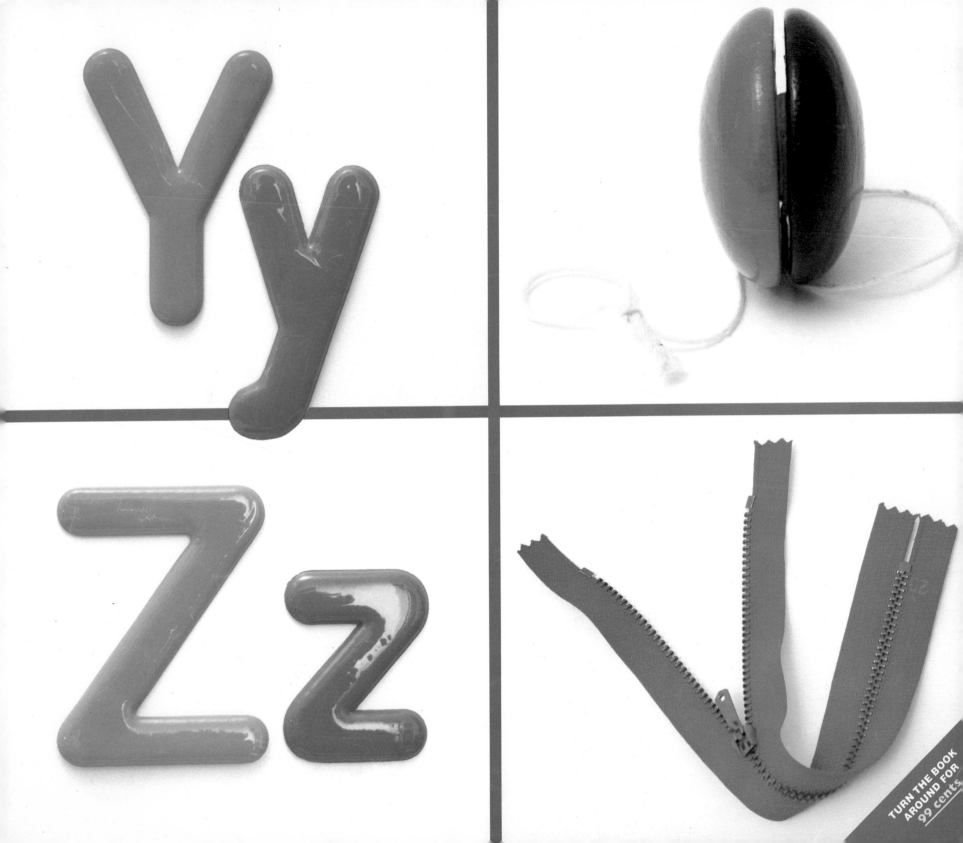

Yy

Zz

TURN THE BOOK AROUND FOR 99 cents

26

25

22

21

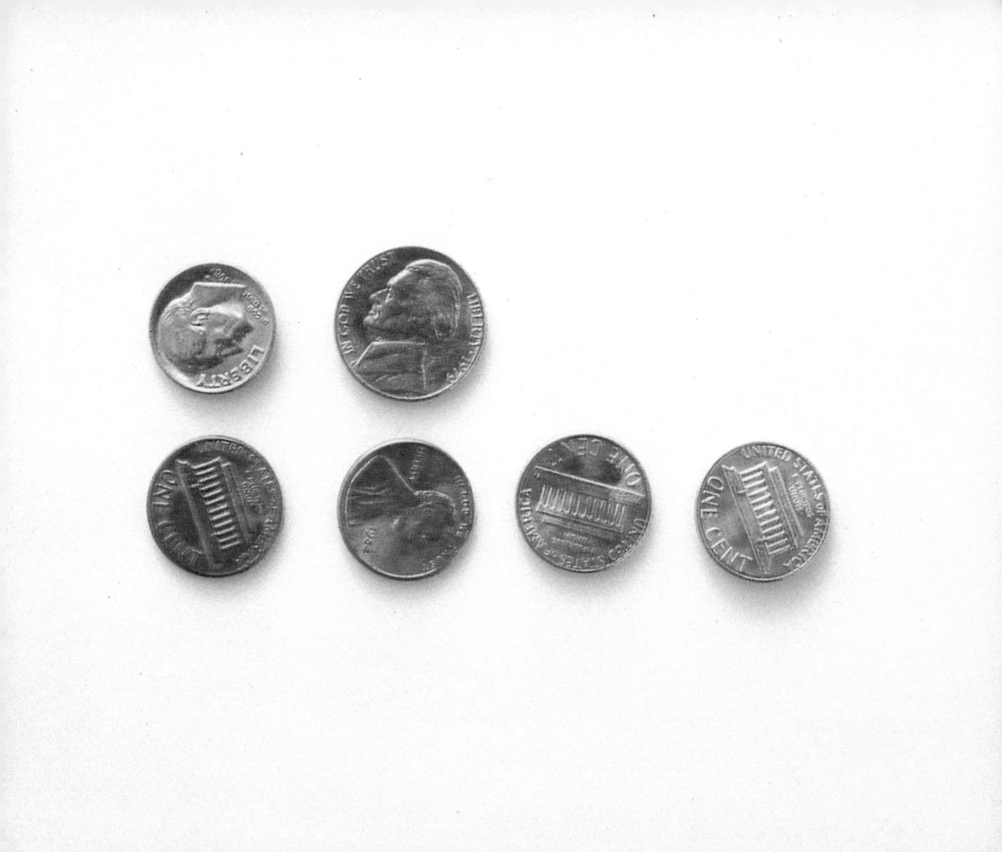

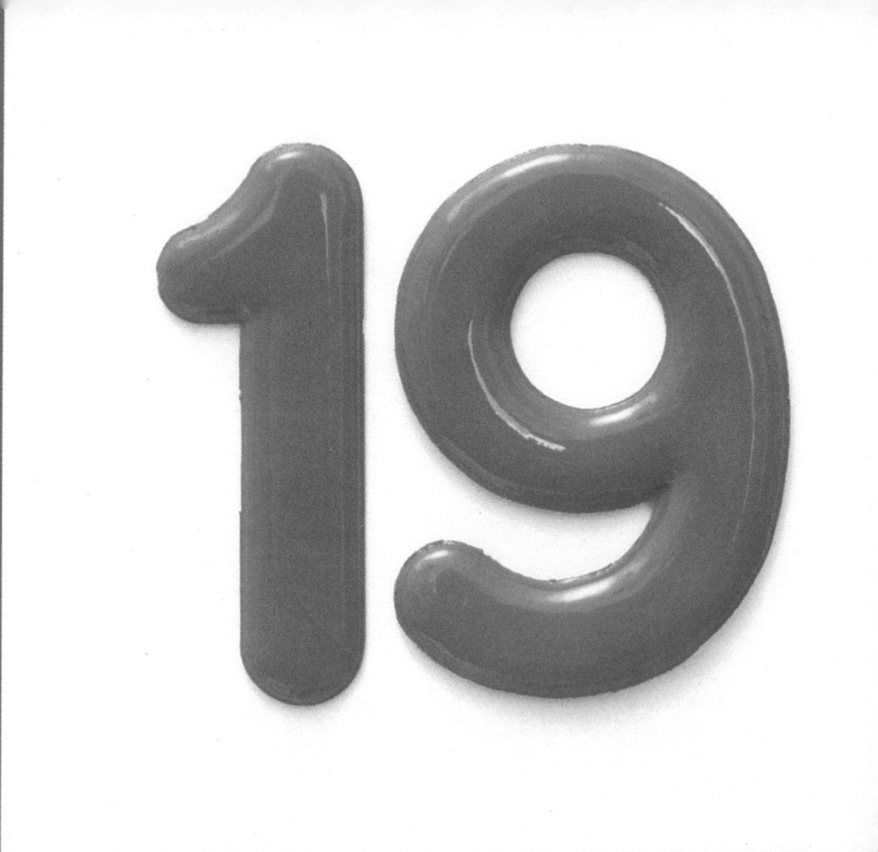
19

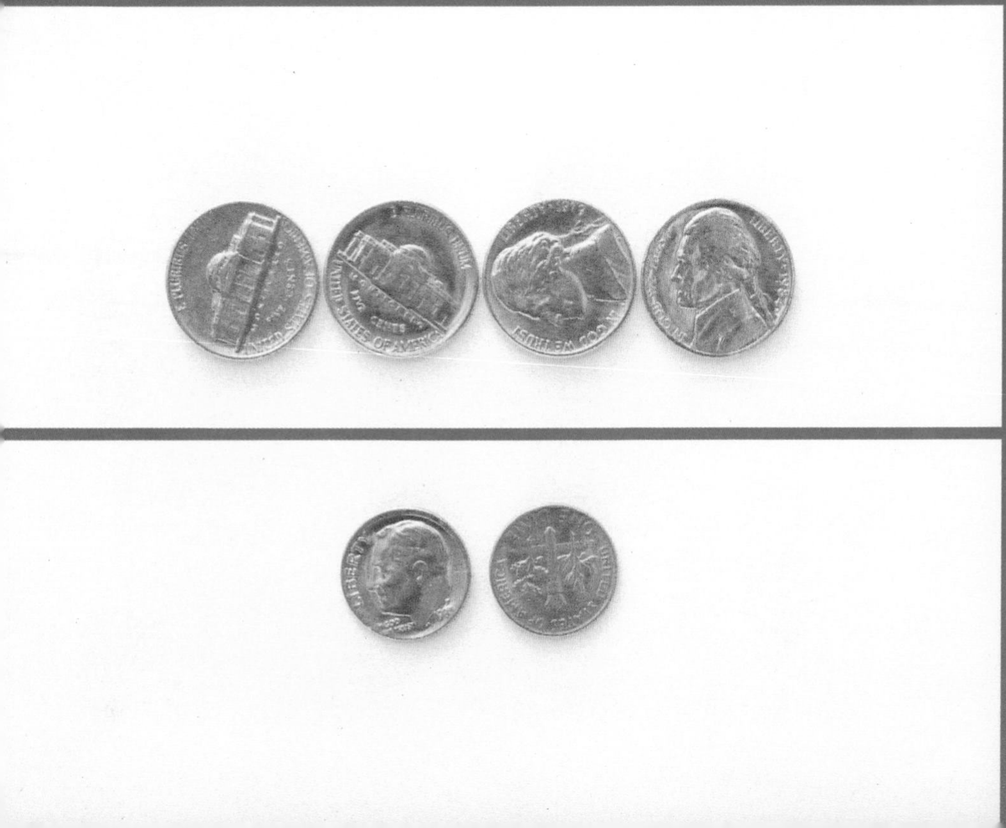

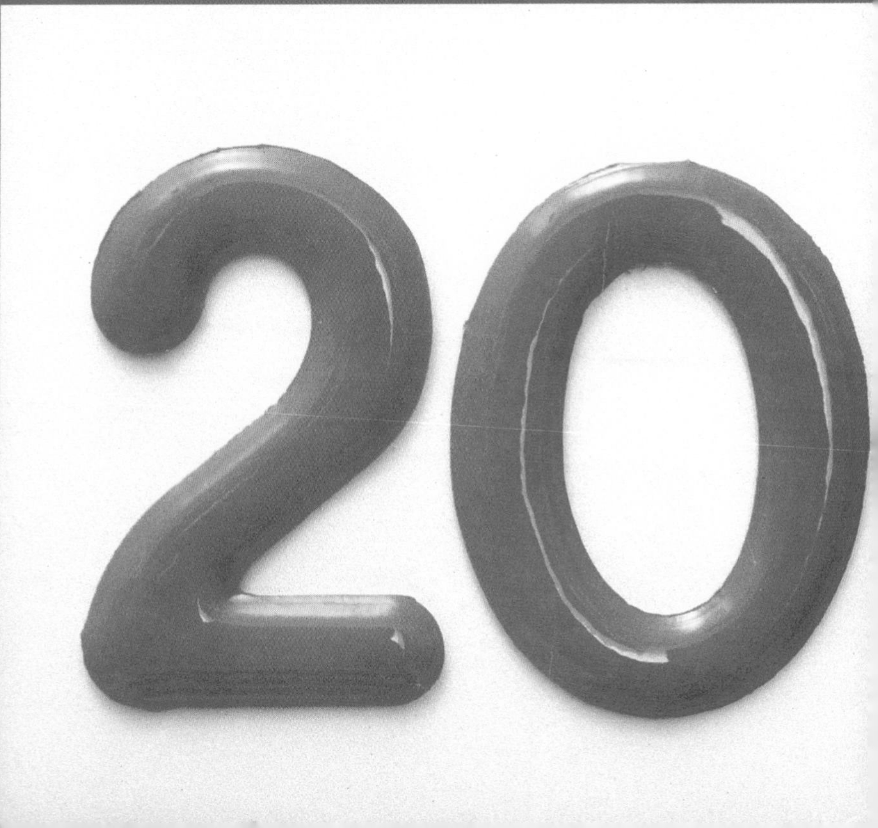
20

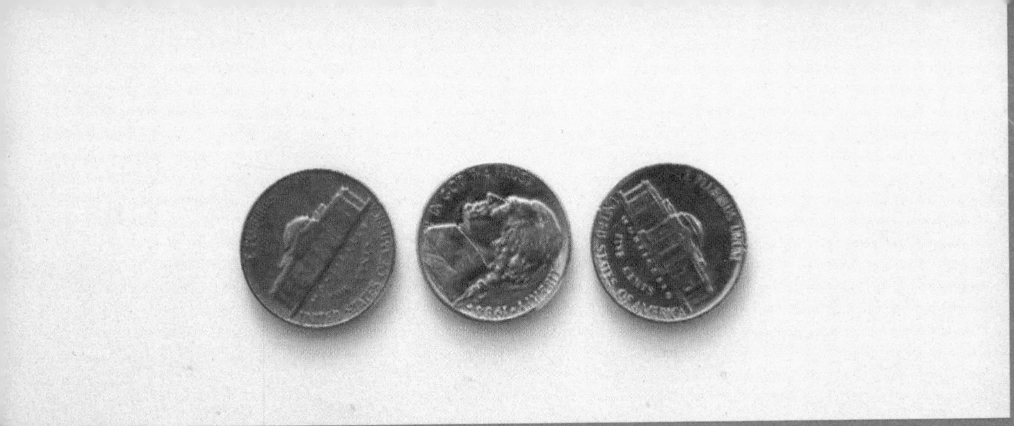

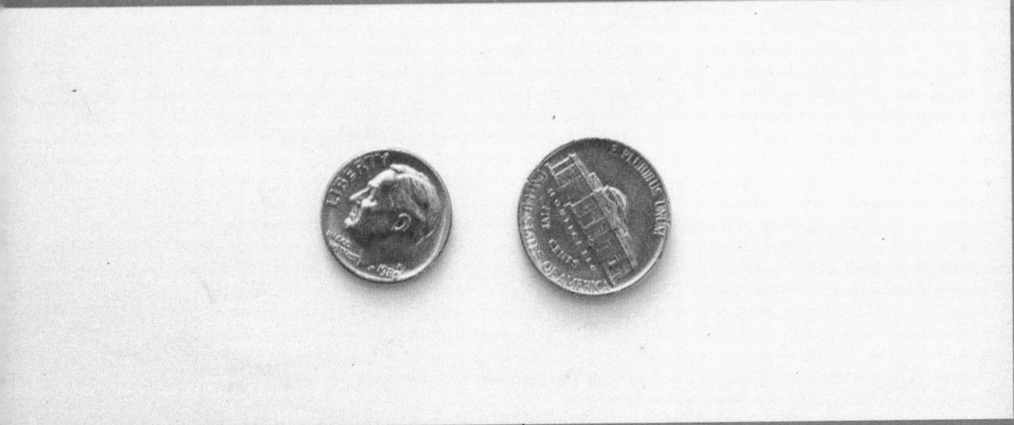

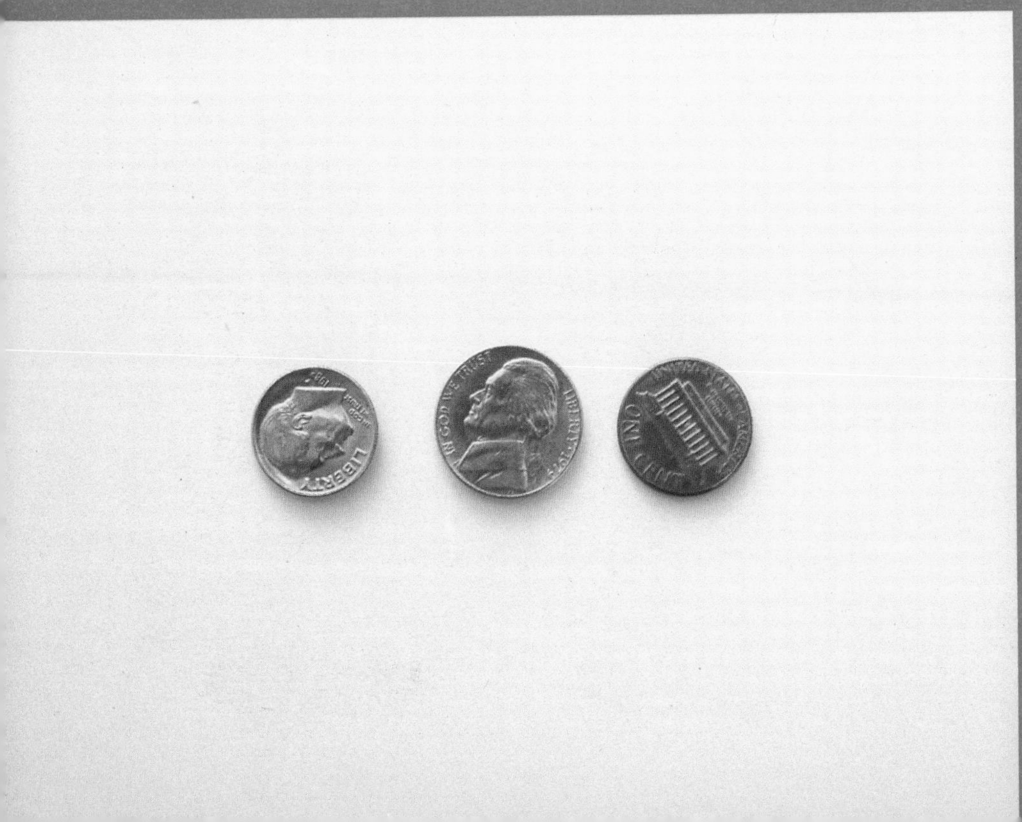

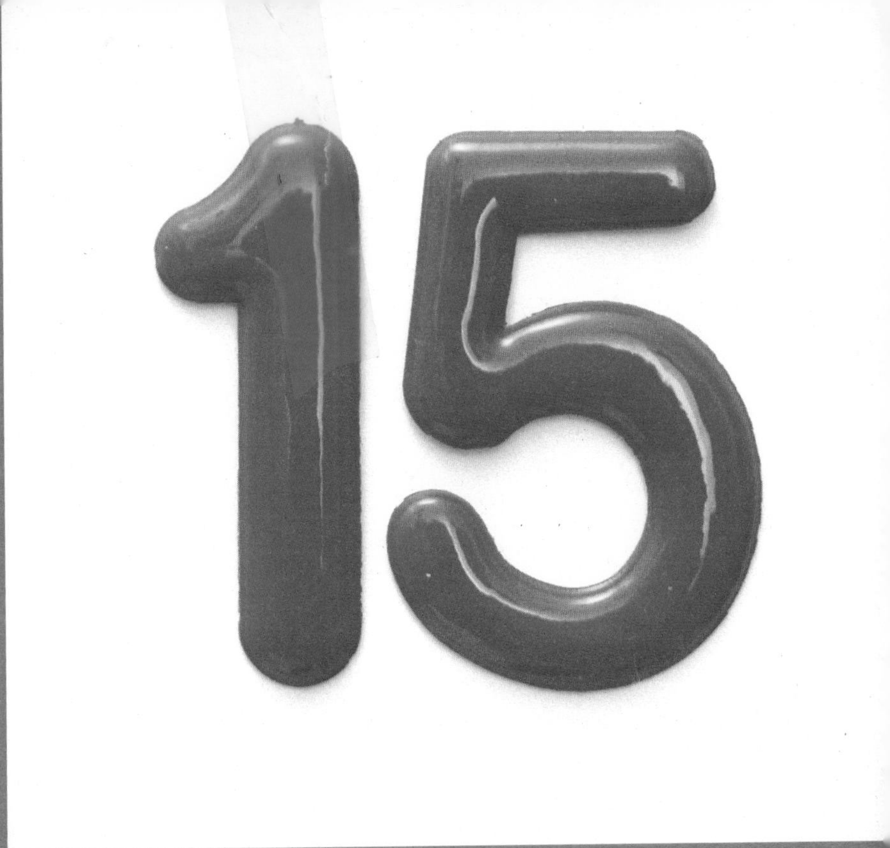
15

16

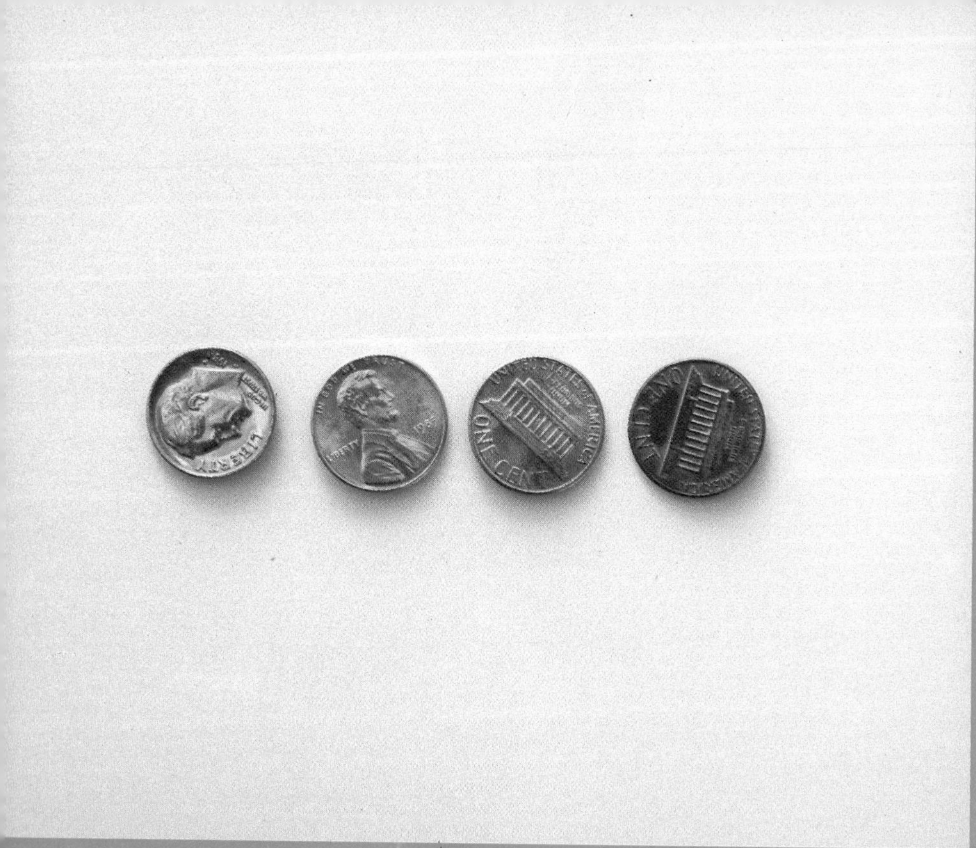

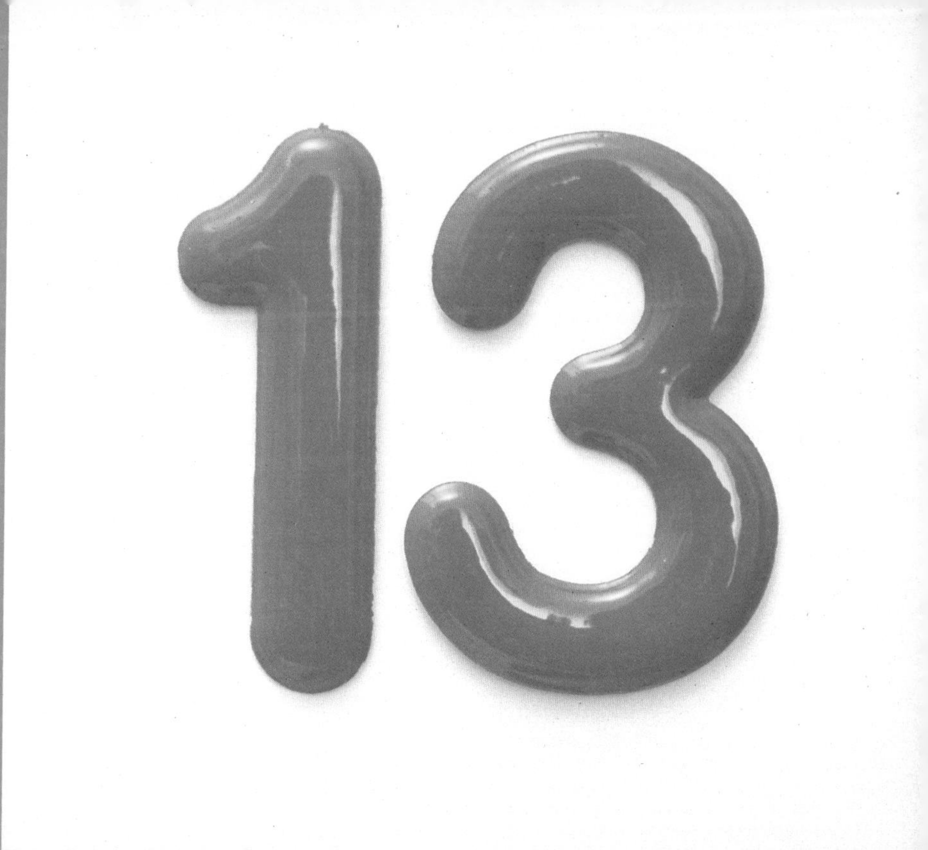
13

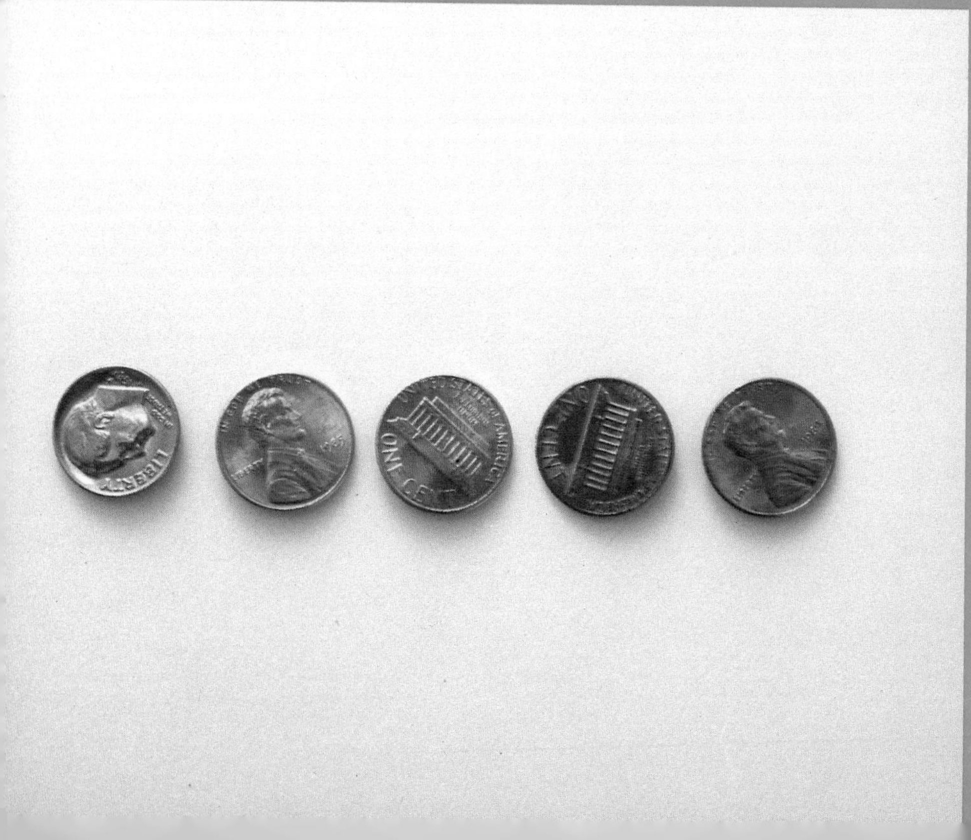

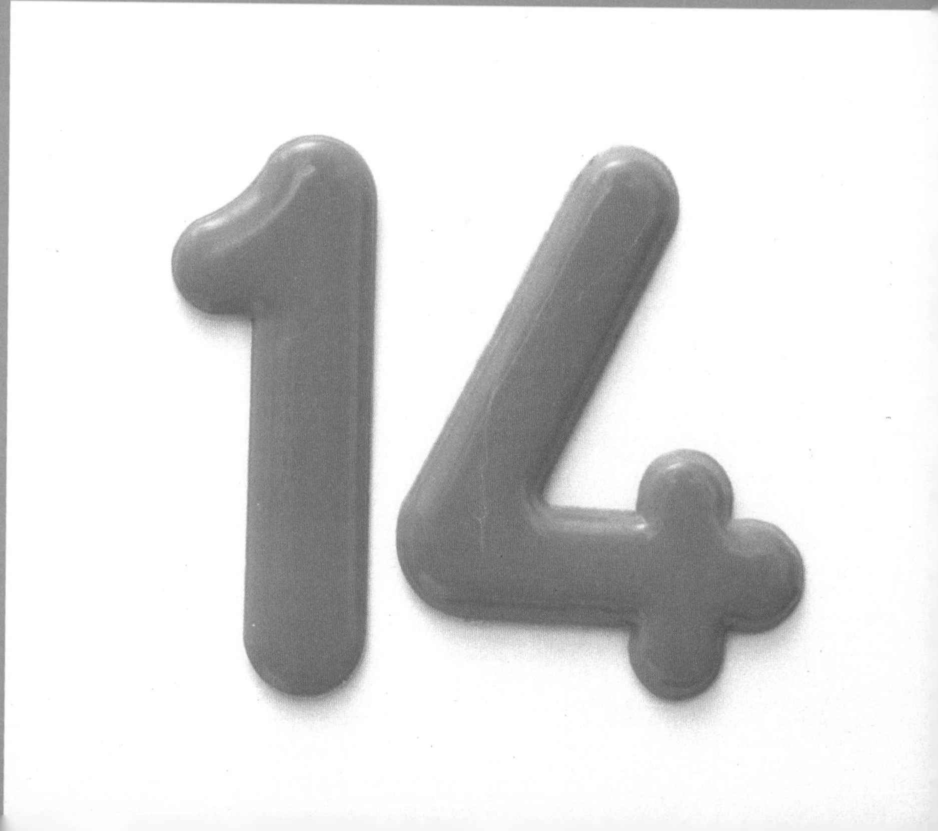
14

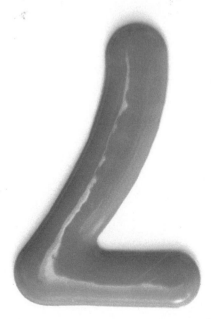

This one is for Candace

Soft Touch letters and numbers used in this book are available at most toy stores.

The photographs were reproduced from 35-mm slides and printed in full color.

The Library of Congress has cataloged the Greenwillow Books edition of *26 Letters and 99 Cents* as follows: Hoban, Tana. 26 letters and 99 cents. Summary: Color photographs of letters, numbers, coins, and common objects introduce the alphabet, coinage, and the counting system.
ISBN 0-688-06361-6 ISBN 0-688-06362-4 (lib. bdg.)
1. English language—Alphabet—Juvenile literature.
2. Counting—Juvenile literature.   [1. Alphabet.
2. Counting. 3. Coins] I. Title. II. Title: Twenty-six letters and ninety-nine cents.
PE1155.H57 1987 [E] 86-11993

10 9 8 7 6 5 4
First Mulberry Edition, 1995
ISBN 0-688-14389-X

26 letters and 99 cents

BY TANA HOBAN

A MULBERRY PAPERBACK BOOK, NEW YORK

MULBERRY BOOKS